W9-AKC-721

STEP INTO READING® will help your child get there. The program offers five steps to reading success. Each step includes fun stories and colorful art or photographs. In addition to original fiction and books with favorite characters, there are Step into Reading Non-Fiction Readers, Phonics Readers and Boxed Sets, Sticker Readers, and Comic Readers—a complete literacy program with something to interest every child.

Learning to Read, Step by Step!

Ready to Read   Preschool–Kindergarten
• big type and easy words • rhyme and rhythm • picture clues
For children who know the alphabet and are eager to begin reading.

Reading with Help   Preschool–Grade 1
• basic vocabulary • short sentences • simple stories
For children who recognize familiar words and sound out new words with help.

Reading on Your Own   Grades 1–3
• engaging characters • easy-to-follow plots • popular topics
For children who are ready to read on their own.

Reading Paragraphs   Grades 2–3
• challenging vocabulary • short paragraphs • exciting stories
For newly independent readers who read simple sentences with confidence.

Ready for Chapters   Grades 2–4
• chapters • longer paragraphs • full-color art
For children who want to take the plunge into chapter books but still like colorful pictures.

STEP INTO READING® is designed to give every child a successful reading experience. The grade levels are only guides; children will progress through the steps at their own speed, developing confidence in their reading. The F&P Text Level on the back cover serves as another tool to help you choose the right book for your child.

Remember, a lifetime love of reading starts with a single step!

*For my parents, Gladys and Steve, who have
always made every holiday memorable*
—N.K.

For my boys, Felix and Bailey
—M.D.

This is how you say the words in this book:
Dreidel: DRAY-dul
Hanukkah: HAH-nuh-kuh
Latkes: LOT-kuhs
Maccabees: MAK-uh-beez
Menorah: muh-NOR-uh
Miracle: MEER-uh-kul
Sufganiyot: soof-gah-nee-OAT

Text copyright © 2021 by Nancy Krulik
Cover art and interior illustrations copyright © 2021 by Monique Dong

All rights reserved. Published in the United States by Random House Children's Books, a division of Penguin Random House LLC, New York.

Step into Reading, Random House, and the Random House colophon are registered trademarks of Penguin Random House LLC.

Visit us on the Web!
StepIntoReading.com
rhcbooks.com

Educators and librarians, for a variety of teaching tools, visit us at RHTeachersLibrarians.com

Library of Congress Cataloging-in-Publication Data is available upon request.
ISBN 978-0-593-37584-6 (trade) — ISBN 978-0-593-37586-0 (lib. bdg.) —
ISBN 978-0-593-37585-3 (ebook)

Printed in the United States of America   10 9 8 7 6 5 4 3 2 1   First Edition

This book has been officially leveled by using the F&P Text Level Gradient™ Leveling System.

IS IT HANUKKAH YET?

by Nancy Krulik

illustrated by Monique Dong

Random House 🏠 New York

Today is Hanukkah!
I cannot wait to
light the candles
and play the games.

"Not yet," says Grandma.
"We have to wait
for the sun to set."

Waiting is hard.
While we wait,
we find my favorite
menorah.

Hanukkah lasts
for eight nights.
We will light one
candle for each night.

Today,

I put two candles

in place.

One is for the
first night
of Hanukkah.
The second candle
lights the first one.

Grandpa fries
potato pancakes.
We call them latkes.
I cannot wait to eat one.

"Not yet,"
    says Grandpa.
"We have to wait
    for the sun to set."

Grandma and I
are making
a surprise for
Mommy and Daddy.

We sing our special song while we work. I love singing with Grandma.

Grandpa tells me
the story of the
Hanukkah miracle.

The Maccabees
had oil
to light their menorah
for only one day.
But the oil lasted
for eight days!

Jingle, jangle.

I hear a key
in the lock.
I run to the door.

Daddy is home!

Mommy too!

I look outside.

It is dark.

"The sun has set!"
I shout.
"Is it Hanukkah yet?"

Daddy gives me
a great big hug.
"It sure is!"
he says.

No more waiting.

Grandma lights
the candles.
I help say the prayers.

We play the dreidel game.

Whee!

All the candy

is for me!

We sing about a dreidel
made of clay.
I spin and spin,
just like a dreidel.

Grandma gives me a gift.

Wow!
It is the music box
we play with
at her house.

"Happy Hanukkah!"
Grandma says.
"Now you can
hear our special song
anytime you like!"

We eat Grandpa's latkes
with our Hanukkah
dinner.
Then it is time
for the surprise.

Sufganiyot for dessert!

Daddy takes
a big bite
of a special
Hanukkah doughnut.

Squirt!

A big glob of jelly
lands on his chin.
He licks it right up.
Silly Daddy.

Do you know
what I like best
about Hanukkah?

Hanukkah lasts for
eight days!
So I get to
do it all again.
I just have to
wait for tomorrow.